Very Little Sleeping Beauty's tower
Very Little Red Riding Hood lives HERE! (and her Mommy) (and Red Teddy)
The Woods!
Very Little Jack's house
Grandma's house
LOOK!
STOP!
lovely flowers here signed wolf
No WOLVES HONEST!
Very Little Cinderella's house
Babysitter needed. Quick

Very little Sleeping Beauty

Teresa Heapy & Sue Heap

Houghton Mifflin Harcourt
Boston New York

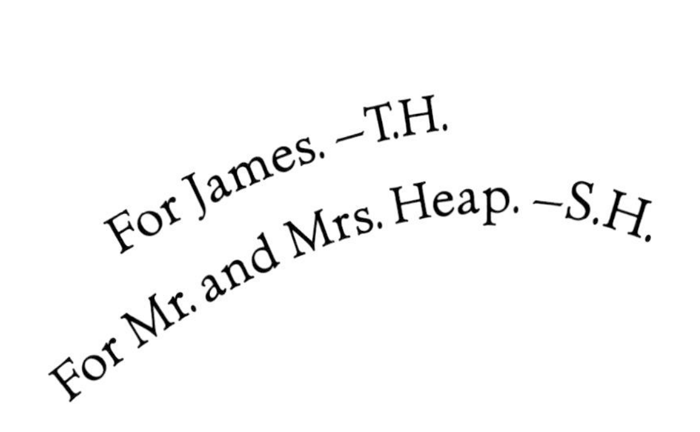

For James. –T.H.
For Mr. and Mrs. Heap. –S.H.

Originally published in Great Britain by Picture Corgi,
an imprint of Random House Children's Publishers UK, 2016.

www.hmhco.com

The text of this book is set in OPTI Adminster Book.
The illustrations are watercolor and ink.

ISBN 978-0-544-28279-7

Manufactured in China
TOP 10 9 8 7 6 5 4 3 2 1

4500568912

It was bedtime.
But Very Little Sleeping Beauty
was not feeling very tired.

Tomorrow was her birthday.
"I going to have party, with cake and Aunty Fairy," said **Very** Little Sleeping Beauty.

"Yes, yes," said her Daddy. "Mummy's making your cake, Aunty Fairy's wrapping you a present, and tonight . . .

. . . you need to go to bed EARLY."

"OK, my Daddy,"
said Very Little Sleeping Beauty.
"But first . . . we *have* to have a song!"

"I see," said her Daddy. "A lullaby?"

"Oh, no," said Very Little Sleeping Beauty.
"A proper sing-song song!"

So her Daddy sang

"She'll Be Coming Round the Mountain."

He sang

"Oh, I Do Like to Be Beside the Seaside."

He sang

"Boom-a-Bap-a-Bing-Bong-Bed!"

"And NOW, it's **bedtime**,"
said her Daddy.

"Oh, NO," said Very Little
Sleeping Beauty.

"Now we need to have . . .

stories,

and tickles,

and dancing,

and a jump on the bed!”

"But NOW it's **bedtime**," said her Daddy.

"Oh, **not yet**, my Daddy," said Very Little Sleeping Beauty.

"Because . . ."

I need my *bear*,
and my *blanket*,

Very Little Sleeping Beauty's
Daddy couldn't find the special cup.

He was gone a
l o n g time.

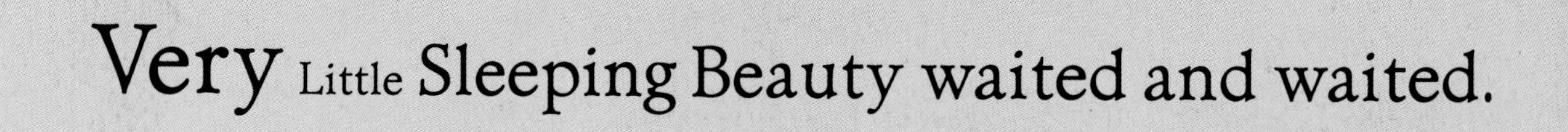

Very Little Sleeping Beauty waited and waited.

"My DADDY!" she sang. "**Where are you?**
Are you and Mummy and Aunty Fairy playing
a hide-and-seek game?
I coming to **find** you!"

So **Very** Little Sleeping Beauty
went to look for everyone.

She looked all around the castle.

And then at last, at the top of the tallest tower, Very Little Sleeping Beauty spied a door.

She c-r-e-a-k-e-d it open,

and there was . . .

Aunty Fairy.

"Hello, my dear," said Aunty Fairy.

"Ooooh – a present!"

said Very Little Sleeping Beauty.

"For me?"

"Yes, my dear," said Aunty Fairy.
"I wanted to give you a **special** gift."

Very Little Sleeping Beauty ripped open the present.

"A wheel!" she said.

"For driving!

Does it have a beeper?"

"Er, no," said Aunty Fairy.
"It's a spinning wheel.
Be careful of the needle!"

"A big wheel!" said Very Little Sleeping Beauty. "Get out of the way!

I do driving!"

Very Little Sleeping Beauty twisted
and turned the spinning wheel . . .

and suddenly . . .

it **broke**,

in pieces,

all over the floor.

Aunty Fairy was **very upset.**

"Look at your lovely spinning wheel, all BROKEN!" she yelled.

Very Little Sleeping Beauty burst into tears. Her Daddy heard her. He ran into the room.

"She b-broke the spinning wheel!" sobbed Aunty Fairy.

"She yelled at me!" sobbed **Very** Little Sleeping Beauty.

Her Daddy looked at them both. "It's late. We're all **very** tired," he said.

"I want **both** of you to say sorry."

"I'm sorry!" said Aunty Fairy. "And I'm sorry more!" said **Very** Little Sleeping Beauty.

"All right," said her Daddy.

"And **now** . . .

it really is

bedtime!"

Very Little Sleeping Beauty's Daddy gave her a hug.
He carried her back to her room.

He got her blanket, her drink, and her bear.
He sang and he read and he smoothed out her hair.

Then **Very** Little Sleeping Beauty's Daddy gave her a kiss.

And at last, just as the sun was about to rise, **Very** Little Sleeping Beauty fell asleep.

She slept and she slept, all day,
until the time for her party came – and went.

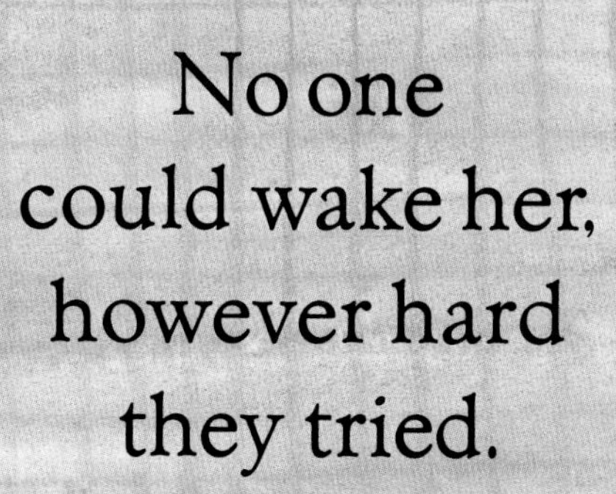

No one
could wake her,
however hard
they tried.

And then, when it was time to go to bed again, Very Little Sleeping Beauty woke up.

"I have party!" she said.

So Very Little Sleeping Beauty had a

pyjama party!

There was ice cream,

and cake,

and jumping,

and swinging.

There were dances, and games,

and bouncing, and singing.

And
they all partied
happily ever
after.

Night-night!

Night-night!

Night-night!